Amber Was Brave,

Essie Was Smart

The story of Amber and Essie told here
in POEMS and PICTURES
by

Vera B Williams

GREENWILLOW BOOKS
An Imprint of HarperCollins*Publishers*

About commas, capitals, periods . . .

In all my other books I have used capitals to begin
sentences; periods, question marks, exclamation marks
to end them; and commas, colons, semicolons, and
quotation marks where expected.

Here I have used those marks more freely (and
less often), as suits my poetry and this story.

—V. B. W.

Amber Was Brave, Essie Was Smart
Copyright © 2001 by Vera B. Williams
All rights reserved. Manufactured in China by
South China Printing Company Ltd.
www.harperchildrens.com

Colored pencils were used to prepare the full-color art.
The black-and-white drawings were done with a black pencil.
The typefaces used are Cochin and ITC Garamond Italic.

Library of Congress Cataloging-in-Publication Data

Williams, Vera B.
Amber was brave, Essie was smart / written and illustrated by Vera B. Williams.
    p.   cm.
"Greenwillow Books."
Summary: Two sisters help each other deal with life while
their mother is working and their father has been sent to jail.
ISBN 0-06-029460-4 (trade). ISBN 0-06-029461-2 (lib. bdg.)
ISBN 0-06-057182-9 (pbk.)
[1. Sisters—Fiction.] I. Title.
PZ7.W6685 Am 2001   [Fic]—dc21   00-048438
First Edition 20 19 18 17 16 15 14 13 12

Contents

Introducing
Amber and Essie
4 PORTRAITS

AMBER

ESSIE

Amber and Essie
POEMS AND
DRAWINGS

Amber Was Brave, Essie Was Smart

Amber could write her name in script
Essie taught her
But Essie could read hard library books
Amber could tie her own shoes
if Essie double tied them for her
Essie could thread a needle
cook toasted cheese sandwiches
make cocoa
put the lipstick on just right
when they played dress-up
Amber was brave

She could get the grocery man
to trust them for a container of milk
though their mother
couldn't pay him till payday
Amber wasn't afraid of the rat
in the wall under the sink
or of climbing up in high places
Essie kept their house key in her little purse
but the front door to their building wouldn't even open
unless they both pushed on it hard
Essie was tall and Amber was small
Essie was smart and Amber was brave
Essie and Amber
Amber and Essie ◇

Best Sandwich

"Best Sandwich" they called it
with Amber on one side
and Essie on the other
with one fat pillow close by Essie's cheek
and one fat pillow by Amber's
while Wilson The Bear
lay right in the middle
up against them both

"Best Sandwich" they called it
and it filled them up
when peanut butter wouldn't
and jelly couldn't
(only crackers were on the shelf anyway)
when their Mama was at her job
and their Daddy was far away
and the house felt dark

When they did "Best Sandwich"
it turned the room friendly from strange
and they could breathe each other's breath
in and out and in and out
till they heard at last
their mother's key in the big front door >

Essie and Amber Tell Who Takes Care of Them

Sundays our mother takes care of us
the whole day
and Saturday afternoons
if she doesn't have to work
But Saturdays we take care of ourselves a lot
Essie says she really takes care of Amber
(but Amber says, Remember, Essie,
I take care of you too)
Tuesdays and Thursdays
is Helen downstairs
Her apartment smells funny, Amber says,
but she makes good macaroni and cheese
Mondays and Wednesdays
after school
we go to Mimi our big cousin
She plays cards with us
and boy do we dance
when she isn't talking to her best friend Russell
on the phone
But she hangs up finally
when it turns dark so suddenly
like in autumn
Then she walks us all the way home ◇

The Question That Always Made Amber Cry

Amber had a question
worse than the meanest mosquito
That question never stopped buzzing
right by her ear
Especially in the early evening
before their mother came home
when Amber had no one to play with
when Essie was deep in her library book
when Wilson The Bear was somewhere under the bed
And even though Amber knew for sure
that Essie would yell at her
never to ask that question again
the question's evil power
forced Amber to pull Essie's hands from her ears
and beg,
Tell me just one more time, Essie . . .
Where is Daddy? ◇

Remember we were right in the kitchen
when the cops came,
Essie insisted
Remember we saw them
take Daddy down the stairs
Remember we watched from behind the curtain
till we couldn't find that cop car anymore
Remember how Mommy cried and then she told us
how Daddy lost his job . . .
how Daddy needed money . . .
how he forged the check . . .
how he signed his boss's name . . .
how the bank believed he really was the boss
and gave him money that wasn't even his
And *that's* how come forging a check
is *just* the same as stealing
Well it's not *really* stealing, Amber said,
and Daddy is *not* bad
It is *too* stealing, Essie told Amber,
and it's *very* bad
That's why the judge sentenced Daddy to jail
And *even* though Mommy says not to tell anyone
and *even* if you ask about it a million times more
that won't change it

Well if you say that
you can't be my sister anymore, Amber said,
while she wriggled away under the bed
to find Wilson ◇

Conversation Under the Bed

Amber lay on her back
and held Wilson on her tummy
with her hand behind his head
so they could really talk together

Daddy is *not* bad is he,
she asked Wilson
And Wilson shook his head for No
but Amber was still crying

Daddy is good isn't he,
Amber asked Wilson
She was still crying
but she nodded Wilson's head for Yes

Daddy couldn't really be bad
because he's *my* daddy, Amber said,
only crying a little still
and she and Wilson shook his head for No

And he'll come back
and everything will be all right
isn't that right, she said,
and she made Wilson nod Yes Yes Yes
Then Amber stopped crying
and hugged Wilson hard ⟨⟩

Essie the Good Sister

Amber came out from under the bed
dragging Wilson
Essie had fixed cocoa and toast
and though there was nothing good to spread
on the toast
Essie cut it into triangles
to dip in their cocoa
Essie helped Amber brush under-the-bed stuff
off of Wilson's fur
Essie wiped the tear stains
from Amber's cheeks
with a piece of crumpled toilet paper from her pocket
Then Amber said Essie could be her sister again
and she made Wilson nod Yes
Of course Yes because he knew
it would always be Amber and Essie
Essie and Amber ◇

No I Won't/Yes I Will

Show it to me,
Essie said

              No, Amber said

Come on
Show it to me

              I won't

You have to

              But I can't

I'll get it
I'll stand on the dresser
I'm taller

              I don't care

              You can't see it

Why not

              Because

Because why

              It's a poem

So?

              It's a silly poem

So?

              OK I'll read it to you

              But you have to shut your eyes ◇

Daddy Song

*D*addy

Sadly

Daddy

Badly

Daddy

Bigly

Daddy

Minely

Daddy

Whenly

Daddy

Really

Really

Soonly ⟩

On the ground floor was Mr. Ashford
He owned the whole house
The first floor was Helen
        And then us,
        said Amber
Third floor was Mr. and Mrs. Avakian
so quiet Essie called them
The Silents
but no one at all
lived on the top floor
            Because it's hot in the summer,
            their mother said,
            and cold in the winter
        But it has a turret, Amber said
        And from that turret
        you can see the whole world
        Let's move up there, said Amber
            I think we'll stay right where we are thank you,
            said their mother

So #5 stayed dark and empty
till one day . . .
just as the sun was setting
a table and chairs
two beds
and a man came up the stairs
and a box of what looked like pots and pans
with a clock on top
followed by a girl ◇

Top of the Stairs

One potato two potato
three potato four
five potato six potato
seven potato more
O U T spells out
and out you go
But Essie said she would not go first
Amber was braver
so Amber would have to
There were twelve steps
and then a bend
where the carpet ended
and then two more
up to the light green door

Essie says,
That girl must have been standing
right behind that door
waiting for us
Before we could even ring the bell
out she came
and closed the door
real fast behind her
Hi, she said,
I'm Nata-Lee
Two words with a dash
Nata-Lee ‹›

Little Song by Amber

*L*isten to my song,
Amber asked Essie
Sure, said Essie,
but don't sing too loud
and not right there
right in my ear

One day a beautiful girl came
And if you ask me
I'll even tell you her name
Lee   it's Lee   it's Nata-Lee
So go and look and you will see
Two beds   two chairs
A table there
Look and look
It's all you'll see
In the turret home of
Nata-Lee ◇

Late

*I*t was late
and their mother wasn't home yet
After supper the radiator got cold
and they were shivery
But then Essie and Amber
and Wilson between them
in "Best Sandwich"
were warming up
with Amber's breath
right by Essie's ear
Do you really think
she lives there all alone,
Amber whispered
Kids can't live all alone,
Essie told her
Yes they can if they're brave and smart
and they can cook,
Amber whispered back
What about money silly, Essie said
You don't know everything, Amber told her
But I know *that*, Essie said,
and anyway she *does* have a daddy
only he works real late ⟨⟩

Sad Lullaby

*E*ssie's sleeping
Amber's watching
Their mother
Sitting   sitting
Just sitting
On her bed

Essie's sleeping
Amber's listening
To the sighing   sighing
And the turning this way
Turning that way
From her mother's bed

Essie's waking
To Amber crying
Now she's reaching out her arm
And rocking   rocking
Essie's rocking Amber
Back to sleep ⟨⟩

At the Table in Nata-Lee's Turret House

Amber and Essie brought

their two apples

to share with Nata-Lee

who asked if they ever

saw the star

inside an apple

These are just apples

from the store,

Amber warned Nata-Lee,

so she wouldn't be disappointed

But Nata-Lee grabbed a knife

and cut the apple right across

Across the equator, Essie said,

like you cut an orange

And there was the star

with the little seeds

tucked down in

like eyes just showing

Two stars

One in each half

Four stars in two apples

divided between three people

equals one and a third stars

for each of us to eat, Essie said

And they ate them very slowly ◇

Knowledge

*E*ssie knows 1/3 and 1/2 and 1/8

She even knows 1/16

She knows the equator and continents

and how the world began

Essie is my sister

and she knows everything, said Amber

Nata-Lee said, Only God

knows everything

How do you know, asked Amber

Because that's where my mother is,

said Nata-Lee . . . with God ◇

Whoops

Amber is jumping on the bed
Now Essie is too
and that makes Wilson bounce
till Amber bounces higher
which nose-dives Wilson to the floor
Amber hits the ceiling with her fingers
Essie hits it with her hair
Down they come
First Amber
then Essie on top of her
WATCH OUT,
shrieks Amber,
as the bed
goes crashing to the floor
squashing poor Wilson flat
But Essie and Amber
can't stop laughing
Look how far away the ceiling
We're in a field
and that's the sky ◇

Emergency Adventure

*E*ssie is smart
She told Amber to say
it was an emergency
Amber is brave
She went right up
to ask the Avakians if she could please
use their phone because, she explained,
ours is turned off
till my mother can pay the bill

We have an emergency,
Amber told their Uncle Eddie B.
who asked like he always asked,
Who broke what this time
Still he promised
to come fix it
It'll be just like new, he said,
only not till tomorrow

Then Amber ran like anything
all the way up to the turret
to invite Nata-Lee to spend the night
camping out with her and Essie and Wilson
in their bed on the floor
with the ceiling for the sky ◇

Thursday Afternoon with Amber and Essie

*H*elen downstairs had a splitting headache

so Amber and Essie went home

We can have a snack, Amber whispered,

and wait for Mommy

But there were only a few flakes

left in the cereal box

Not even half a glass

was in the milk container

And the last banana

was brown

Brown and leaky

Wouldn't it be great,

Amber asked Essie,

if you could squeeze a milk carton

like an orange

so you could get more milk

even when it's empty

You mean like THAT, said Essie,

as she squashed the empty container flat

with her foot

and kicked it hard at the garbage pail ‹›

Amber Wants to Talk

Amber told Wilson The Bear
that she was so mad at Essie
she could burst
because Essie wouldn't talk to her
and wouldn't and wouldn't
So then Amber said, OK she wouldn't
say a single word to Essie either
and see how Essie liked *that*
Only Essie had a new library book
so she never even looked up
from the page once
or heard when Amber asked
in a really little voice,
Essie don't you think
it's awfully awfully quiet in here ◇

Amber Decides an Important Thing

*I*t's true
Amber wasn't paying attention
so her jacket *was* buttoned all wrong
And that's why Essie said,
Come here Stupid
I'll fix it for you
That's when Amber put her fists on her waist
She marched herself right up close
in front of Essie
IF YOU CALL ME STUPID ONE MORE TIME,
she told Essie,
I'LL GO BE NATA-LEE'S SISTER
OK *Stoopid*, said Essie,
and she grabbed Amber around the middle
and lifted her right off the floor
and dumped her on the bed
to tickle her till she laughed
because Essie was tall
while Amber was small ◇

*E*ssie said she would try

to get it straight all the way around

But you know, she said,

since you tried to cut a star from the soup can

with Mommy's good scissors

they won't hardly cut hair anymore

But Amber was crying

so Essie pushed her right

up close to the mirror

and she snipped and cut all around

Hey you're making it even shorter, Amber yelled

But it's getting more even, Essie told her

Anyway I think it's cute

Mommy won't think so, Amber said

She's always saying how she loves my braids

Only I had to cut them off,

Amber said,

to send to Daddy

so he'll be sure to remember me

I had to ◇

Amber's Pleasure

Amber loved to play ball
just when the sun was going away
and the sky turned
the blue that was always
amazing to Amber
Then Amber didn't care
if she was the only person
in the whole world
standing there
right outside the house
throwing a small pink rubber ball
up in the sky
and catching it back
Over
And over
And over again
150, she told Essie
That's my most ever >

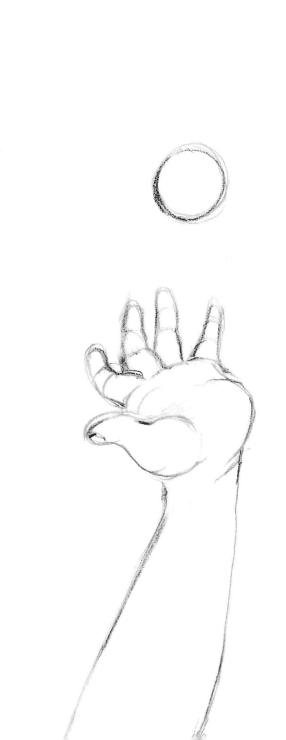

Sunday Beauty Parlor

Sunday just after supper
is Beauty Parlor time at our house
Our mother has a little case
with everything you need
to do nails
We clear everything off the table
and cover it up with a towel
We pull over the lamp
to be very bright
Ma sets out a pot of warm water
filing boards   a nail clipper
a cuticle cutter and a little
pair of scissors with a gold handle
and a bottle of polish
Last Sunday she did Nata-Lee's nails too
Only Ma said there were really
no nails on Nata-Lee you could do
Your poor little hands, my mother said
You've bitten them bloody
Now Nata-Lee won't come to
our Sunday Beauty Parlor anymore ‹›

Strange Day

*I*t was Friday
But they didn't go to Mimi
And they didn't go to Helen
It was only Friday
but their mother stayed home
It's funny today, Amber said
And even Essie agreed
that it was a strange and funny day ⟩

Full Cart

*T*he phone was turned back on
Their mom called up her brother
their Uncle Eddie B.
to meet them at the supermarket

Trailing through the aisles
Amber kept pulling on Essie
to look in the cart
because when their mother
picked up something special
to study the price
she didn't set it back on its shelf
but added it to the cart
till their cart was fuller
than even Essie ever remembered

And again
on the way home
Amber just had to whisper,
Essie   look
Peaches >

Even Before It Got Light

Amber and Essie
are curled in "Best Sandwich"
They don't say a word

It's still only halfway
till morning
But their ears
pick up the music
of their mother's humming
and their feet
transfer it by drumming
on Wilson's furry tummy
cuddled against their toes
at the bottom of the bed ◇

Amber Says What They Did When the Doorbell Rang

I got to the door first

I shut my eyes

I went down the step

One foot

then one foot

One foot

then one foot

One foot . . .

Then I opened my eyes

Daddy was standing right there ›

Amber and Essie

AN ALBUM

BEAUTY PARLOR TIME

NATA-LEE

. . . DOWN THEY COME

I'VE GOT IT

AMBER WITH HER BRAIDS AT HER FEET

ESSIE TRYING TO GET IT STRAIGHT ALL AROUND

ARMS FULL OF GROCERIES

ON THE WAY HOME

AMBER WITH WILSON

AMBER JUMPING

NATA-LEE WITH AMBER AT THE TURRET WINDOW

THE
ATTIC
ROOM OF
NATA-LEE

TICKLE TIME

AMBER

ESSIE

SISTERS